This Book belongs to

....

Princess Pistachio

Marie-Louise Gay

pajamapress

First published in the United States in 2015

Text and illustrations copyright © 2014 Marie-Louise Gay

This edition copyright © 2014 Pajama Press Inc.

Translated from French by Jacob Homel

10 9 8 7 6 5 4 3 2 1

www.pajamapress.ca   info@pajamapress.ca

The publisher gratefully acknowledges the support of the Canada Council for the Arts and the Ontario Arts Council for its publishing program. We acknowledge the financial support of the Government of Canada through the Canada Book Fund for our publishing activities.

Library and Archives Canada Cataloguing in Publication

Gay, Marie-Louise [Princesse Pistache. English]   Princess Pistachio / Marie-Louise Gay ; [translated by Jacob Homel].

Translation of: Princesse Pistache. ISBN 978-1-927485-69-9 (bound)

    I. Homel, Jacob, 1987-, translator II. Title. III. Title: Princesse Pistache. English.

PS8563.A868P7413 2014   jC843'.54   C2014-904891-2

U.S. Publisher Cataloging-in-Publication Data (U.S.)

Gay, Marie-Louise, 1952-

    Princess pistachio / Marie-Louise Gay.

Originally published by Dominique et compagnie: Saint-Lambert, Québec, 1998.

[48] pages : col. ill. ; cm.

Summary: When she receives a mysterious crown for her birthday, Pistachio realizes that she is really an abducted princess. But this only makes her parents sigh, her friends laugh, and her baby sister Penny insist on playing princess, too. When Pistachio's angry wish makes Penny disappear, she needs a princess's courage to get her back.

ISBN-13: 978-1-927485-69-9

1. Humorous stories. 2. Sisters – Juvenile fiction. I. Title.

[E] dc23   PZ7.G39Pr 2014

Cover and book design–Rebecca Buchanan

Manufactured by Qualibre Inc./Print Plus

Printed in China

Pajama Press Inc.

181 Carlaw Ave. Suite 207 Toronto, Ontario Canada M4M 2S1

www.pajamapress.ca

Distributed in Canada by UTP Distribution

5201 Dufferin Street Toronto, Ontario Canada, M3H 5T8

Distributed in the U.S. by Orca Book Publishers

PO Box 468 Custer, WA, 98240-0468, USA

*To Princess Élisa of Quissac
and to her big brother,
the knight Florian.*

• Chapter 1 •
A Real Princess!

Happy birthday, my little princess!

Pistachio can't believe her eyes! She reads and rereads the card that came with the present she found under her bed.

Happy birthday, my little princess! The words dance before her eyes.

"Could it be?" Pistachio thinks.

"Might it be?" Pistachio hopes.

Her heart beats like a drum.

Pistachio unties the ribbon and rips off the paper. A golden crown. A crown for a princess!

"I knew it," Pistachio whispers. "I have always known it! I *am* a princess. A *real* princess!"

All her life, Pistachio believed that her real parents were the king and queen of

a magnificent kingdom. She had found the kingdom on her map of the world. A golden island in the middle of the Indian Ocean—Papua!

The king and queen of Papua adored their little princess. They gave her nothing but chocolates and chestnut ice cream to eat. They dressed her in the finest silks and most delicate ostrich feathers.

Every day, the king and queen
showered her with presents—silver skates,
invisible kites, a parrot that spoke five
languages, and a piano-playing monkey.
A thousand and one presents, each one
more wonderful than the one before.

But one day, a ghastly witch, green
with envy, stole their precious princess.
The witch abandoned her on the
other side of the world, at 23 Maple
Street, with Mr. and Mrs. Shoelace, her
adoptive parents. Ever since that terrible
day, the king and queen of Papua had
desperately searched for her.

"They have found me at last!"
Pistachio sings as she waltzes with her
dog around the room. "They will be
here any day now, to bring me back to
our kingdom. Me, Princess Pistachio of
Papua! Hurray!"

That evening at the dinner table, Pistachio breaks the news to her family. She stands on her chair and proclaims, "I know the whole truth now. From this day forth, you shall call me Princess Pistachio."

Pistachio's mother tries to get Penny to finish another spoonful of creamed spinach. Pistachio's little sister wiggles about like a sea worm and refuses to open her mouth.

"Well." Pistachio's mother sounds a little tired. "How lucky I am to be the mother of a princess."

Penny opens her mouth wide and sprays creamed spinach across the kitchen. "Penny pwincess too!"

The kitchen looks like a Martian battlefield. Spinach runs down the yellow walls, the white tablecloth, and Pistachio's magnificent pink princess dress. Even the dog is a lovely shade of green.

"You are…DISGUSTING!" shouts Princess Pistachio. "You could never be a princess! Besides, you are not even my sister!"

Penny begins to wail. Her face is as red as a beet. It looks quite nice next to the spinachy green.

"Enough!" her father says. "Stop teasing your sister, Pistachio."

"PRINCESS Pistachio," she replies.

"*Miss* Princess Pistachio," her father says, "would you be so kind as to sit down and eat your spinach?"

Princess Pistachio pouts in distaste.

"Princesses," she says, "never eat spinach."

"Princesses," her father replies, "always eat their spinach, or they can't have any dessert."

"I don't care about your crummy dessert!" Pistachio declares as she leaves the kitchen like a real princess: her head held high, her back straight, walking gracefully around the green puddles of spinach.

· Chapter 2 ·
An Angry Princess

The next morning, Pistachio's mother asks her to look after Penny in the garden.

"Can't you see I have other things to do?" Pistachio replies. "Besides, princesses *never* look after smelly babies."

"Princesses," her mother says, "*always* obey their mothers, or they go without television for a week."

"My real mother would never deny me anything," Pistachio mutters.

She sighs and looks at Penny out of
the corner of her eye.

Penny immediately sticks a mud pie
on her head like a crown and hollers, "I
want to pway pwincess!"

Pistachio sticks out her tongue and
turns her back to her little sister. She
adjusts her golden crown and slips on
her white gloves. Now she is ready for
her triumphant tour of the garden.

Princess Pistachio walks with small, delicate steps, like a preening peacock. With a proud smile, she greets the birds on the clothesline. With a tiny nod of her head, she accepts the cheers from a crowd of fawning tulips. Finally, she bows her head and curtsies gracefully before the dog.

"Your Highness," she murmurs. "I am Princess Pistachio of Papua, at your service!"

The dog scratches his ear and yawns hard enough to unhinge his jaw.

Princess Pistachio sighs, again.

Suddenly, she hears a terrible cry. She looks over the fence and sees two dueling knights. Princess Pistachio is horrified: they must be fighting out of love for her!

"I am going to kill you dead, camel head!" Gabriel shouts. His sword tears through the air like lightning.

Jacob dodges the attack. "Missed me again, clucking hen!"

"Stop! I beg of you!" Princess Pistachio cries out.

Surprised, Gabriel and Jacob tumble
to the ground.

"Brave knights, I beg of you!" Princess
Pistachio beseeches. "The last thing
I wish is for one of you to die out of
devotion to me, Princess Pistachio of—"

The two boys look at each other, then
burst out laughing.

"Princess?" Gabriel sniggers. "Even an ugly old toad would want nothing to do with you!"

"To die for a mustachioed pistachi-toad! Ugh!" Jacob cries out.

They run away laughing like monkeys.

"Brutes! Peasants!" Pistachio screams. "I'll feed you to the lions!"

"Eat, dog, eat!" Penny shrieks from behind her.

Princess Pistachio turns around.
Penny is trying to feed tulips to the dog.
Her mother's precious yellow tulips.
    The dog looks green.
    Pistachio sees red.
    She roars, "Penny, you bird brain!"
    Penny wails and turns purple.

· Chapter 3 ·
A Princess at School

On Monday morning, Princess Pistachio's mother shakes her awake.

"Princesses do not go to school," Pistachio mutters and hides under the covers.

"Oh, yes they do!" her mother replies.

"Princesses never get out of bed before noon," Princess Pistachio mumbles as she puts the pillow over her head.

"Oh, yes they do!" her mother insists.

"Princesses never—"

"Do you want me to turn into a horrible witch?" her mother asks. "Or a dragon?"

In a heartbeat, Pistachio jumps out of bed.

Pistachio smiles as she hurries to school. "My friends will be so impressed. I am sure they have never seen a real princess."

Indeed, Princess Pistachio makes quite an impression as she enters the

classroom. Her golden crown sparkles under the neon lights. Her princess gown trails elegantly behind her. Her classmates' eyes are as wide as saucers. Even Mrs. Trumpethead seems at a loss for words. Princess Pistachio sits down next to Madeline, her best friend.

"Why are you wearing such a ridiculous costume?" Madeline whispers. "Halloween is six months away!"

"This is not a costume," Princess Pistachio proudly states. "I *am* a princess. A real princess. I am Princess Pistachio of Papua!"

Princess Pistachio's former best friend begins to giggle uncontrollably.

Madeline giggles so hard that
she does not see Mrs. Trumpethead's
menacing shadow looming over her
desk. Madeline spends the rest of class in
the hallway.

At recess, Princess Pistachio makes a
beeline for Madeline, angry as can be.

"How dare you laugh at me?"

"Pistachio Shoelace! Look at yourself! You are no more a princess than I am. What has got into you? Has a charming prince begged you to try on a glass slipper? Have toads asked you to kiss them?"

"Hummmpf!" Princess Pistachio sneers. "You are jealous. It is clear to me that you do not have a single drop of royal blood in your veins. You—"

Madeline bursts into laughter.

"Princess Pi-Pi-Pistachio of Pa-Pa-Papua! Ha, ha, ha!"

Princess Pistachio whips around and walks away, head held high, a proud smile on her face. But suddenly she trips over her dress, spins around twice, and lands in a huge mud puddle!

All the kids laugh.

Red as a tomato, black with mud, Princess Pistachio wants to cry.

"A princess never cries," she reminds herself and clenches her jaw. "Never, never!"

Fortunately, the recess bell rings.

After her endless day at school, Princess Pistachio slowly makes her way back home. Her beautiful princess dress is covered in mud and clings to her bum. Her crown gives her a headache, and her heart is as heavy as a storm cloud.

Madeline and Chichi speed past her on their skateboards.

"Hey, Pistachio!" Madeline jeers. "How many toads did you kiss today? Ha, ha, ha!"

"Where is your golden carriage?" Chichi teases. "Did it turn into a pumpkin? Ha, ha, ha!"

Princess Pistachio clenches her fists, but does not even look at them. She makes herself a promise—she will show those pumpkin-heads that she is a real princess. Oh, yes, indeed! Her friends will dearly regret making fun of her!

But *how* can she show them?

· Chapter 4 ·
A Princess of Nothing at All

The phone rings as Princess Pistachio walks into her house.

It is her grandfather.

"Hello, my little princess," he says. "Did you receive my present?"

Silence.

"Pistachio?"

"Grandpa?" Princess Pistachio asks in a very small voice. "You…you were the one who sent the crown? You were the one who wrote the card?"

"Yes," her grandfather answers. "But I think I forgot to sign it. Does the crown fit you? Do you like it?"

"It is a wonderful crown," Pistachio replies in an even smaller voice. "Thank you, Grandpa."

"Nothing is too beautiful for my favorite little princess," her grandfather adds. Pistachio hangs up.

Her heart sinks.

She is not a princess.

They were right. She is nothing at all.

Pistachio stares sadly out the window. Out of the corner of her eye, she sees Penny and the dog splashing about in the paddling pool.

Oh no! Pistachio is horrified. She cannot believe her eyes. The dog is wearing her favorite purple blouse and her beautiful red beret! Penny is washing the dog with her magnificent leopard-print scarf!

Pistachio explodes.

She storms out of the house and howls, "PENNEEEY!" She rips the scarf out of her sister's hands. She undresses the dog at full speed.

"The dog is a pwincess!" Penny begins to cry.

"The dog is *not* a princess!" Pistachio rages. "You are *not* a princess! I am the ONLY princess here!"

Pistachio flies up the stairs, slams her bedroom door behind her, and throws herself onto the bed.

"I wish...I wish... Penny would disappear forever!" she cries.

Finally Pistachio falls asleep, her heart as tight as her fists.

· Chapter 5 ·
A Princess in the Dark

It is almost nighttime when Pistachio's father wakes her up.

"Pistachio, is Penny in your room?"

"Of course not," Pistachio says sleepily. "She is not even allowed in here."

"She has disappeared," her father continues. "She was playing with the dog out front…and suddenly she was gone!"

Pistachio blushes. She knows what has happened.

Her wish was granted!

Pistachio jumps out of bed. She must find her sister.

Night has fallen. The whole neighborhood is looking for Penny. Flashlight beams streak across the dark sky like great white ribbons. Worried voices call, "Penny! Penneeey!"

Penny is nowhere to be found.

Pistachio looks all over the house—under the beds, in the cupboards, in the bottom of every sock drawer, behind the fridge, in the fridge, in the attic, in the basement. Everywhere!

No Penny.

Pistachio searches the garden. She is alone. It is as dark as a wolf's den. Her father's tomatoes make faces and whisper to each other. The cauliflowers try to trip her up. Thorny rosebushes grab at her legs.

"A real princess is brave." Pistachio shivers with fear. "I am not very brave, but I have to find Penny. It is my fault that she has disappeared."

Suddenly, a strange noise makes her jump. A loud rumbling growl. It sounds like a snoring dragon. The sound is coming from the far edge of the garden, where the darkest shadows dance.

"Could a d-d-dragon have eaten Penny?" Pistachio wonders as she tiptoes towards the sound. Her hand shakes and her flashlight flickers on and off. The closer she gets to the shadows, the louder the noise becomes. Now it sounds like an entire family of dragons snoring away.

Pistachio fumbles about, trips over some giant roots, and stumbles against the garden shed. She peeks inside.

Penny and the dog are snuggled close together. They are snoring loud enough to wake up any sleeping dragons.

"*Penny*," Pistachio whispers.

Penny opens her eyes. She smiles.
Pistachio holds out her hand.

"Come, Princess Penny. Time to go
home."